Olympic Cycling

Diana Noonan

Contents

Cycling at the Olympic Games

The Olympic and Paralympic Games are two of the most important sports events in the world. Only the best athletes get to take part in them.

Athletes compete in cycling events by riding bikes. Many different cycling events are held at the Olympic and Paralympic Games.

Olympic cycling events take place on racing tracks, trails and roads.

Paralympic cyclists race in a track event.

BMX riders race on a dirt trail.

Olympic cyclists race in a road cycling event.

Mountain Biking

Mountain biking takes place off-road, on rough tracks. There are many different kinds of mountain bike races. At the Olympic Games, the mountain biking event is a cross-country race.

Mountain bikes are strong and light, so riders can go quickly over bumps.

Cross-country mountain bike riders cycle over narrow tracks of grass, dirt and rocks. In wet weather, the tracks can be very slippery. Cross-country bikes have wide, knobbly tyres to help riders stay on the track.

BMX Racing

BMX racing is an Olympic sport.

A BMX race takes place on a course
made up of tricky jumps.
Eight riders take part in each race.

BMX races begin at the top of a hill
so that riders can speed up quickly
as they head down the slope towards the jumps.

BMX riders go over a jump in a race.

Track Cycling

Olympic track cycling takes place
on a 250-metre track called a velodrome.
The track has sloping sides, which make it look
a little like a bowl.
There is a roof over the velodrome.

At the velodrome, crowds sit in the stands and watch the cyclists race.

Track cyclists wear special helmets and tight-fitting clothes called "skinsuits". These help the air to flow more easily past the cyclists as they pedal.

There are six different Olympic track cycling events. Some events test riders' speed. These are the individual **sprint**, the team sprint, and the keirin (say: *keh-rin*).

Some track cycling events test riders' **endurance**. These are the team **pursuit**, the Madison and the omnium (say: *om-nee-um*).

Endurance riders must be able to pedal hard and fast, and to keep going, hour after hour.

Paralympic cyclists race in an individual sprint event.

Individual and Team Sprints

In the individual sprints, two riders at a time race against each other.

The team sprint has two or three riders in each team. Riders in a team take turns to lead for a lap of the velodrome.

After their lap as the leader, each rider leaves the race. Only one rider in each team is left to finish the race.

Individual sprints have only two riders.

Team sprints have two or three riders in each team.

Keirin

In a keirin race, riders cycle six or eight laps of the velodrome.

Keirin riders can go as fast as 70 kilometres per hour.

For the first three laps, riders must stay behind a person on a motorbike. This person is called a "pacer". When the pacer leaves the track, the riders sprint the last three laps to the finish line.

A pacer rides at the front of a keirin race for three laps.

Team Pursuit

The Olympic team pursuit is a 4-kilometre sprint event. It takes place at the velodrome.

Two teams compete in a race, and there are four riders in each team.
Teams start the race on opposite sides of the track.
A team wins by finishing the race in the shortest time, or by overtaking the other team.

Three riders from each team must finish the race.

Olympic team pursuit cyclists race in a velodrome.

Madison

The Madison is a relay sprint event for teams. The two riders in each team take it in turns to race around the track.

The rider who is racing must touch the hand of their waiting teammate. Then, the teammate can start their own lap of the track while the first rider slows down for a rest.

The Madison was named after a huge sports centre in the USA called Madison Square Garden.

RUSSIA
RUSSIA
RUSSIA
RUSSIA
RUSSIA

Omnium

The Olympic omnium is made up of four different track races that all take place in one day. The winner is the rider who has the most points at the end of the day.

All the riders in the omnium races start together in a big group.

The Olympic Road Race

The Olympic road race is an individual event. It can take place on roads in and out of the city where the Olympic Games are being held. Crowds of people line parts of the road to cheer on the riders.

Cycling at the Paralympics

The Paralympic Games are based on the Olympic Games. The event is an international competition for champion athletes who are **disabled**.

Para cyclists take part in track and road events.

Some para cyclists ride two-wheeled bikes. Others ride specially made bikes with three wheels.

Some para cyclists pedal their three-wheeled bikes lying down. Others pedal sitting up.

Some para cyclists use their hands to turn the pedals and steer the bike at the same time.

A tandem is a bike made for two people.

Olympic para cyclists who cannot see very well race on tandems.

Another cyclist rides in the front seat of the tandem to help steer it. This cyclist is called a pilot.

The para cyclist takes care of the speed, while the pilot cyclist steers the tandem.

Olympic and Paralympic cycling events are amazing to watch.

Olympic and Paralympic cyclists are fast, strong and skilful. They train for years for the chance to win an Olympic medal.

Glossary

disabled (*adjective*) unable to do some tasks because of a physical or mental condition

endurance (*noun*) the strength to continue doing something for a long time

pursuit (*noun*) a chase to catch up with something or someone

sprint (*noun*) a short race at full speed

Index